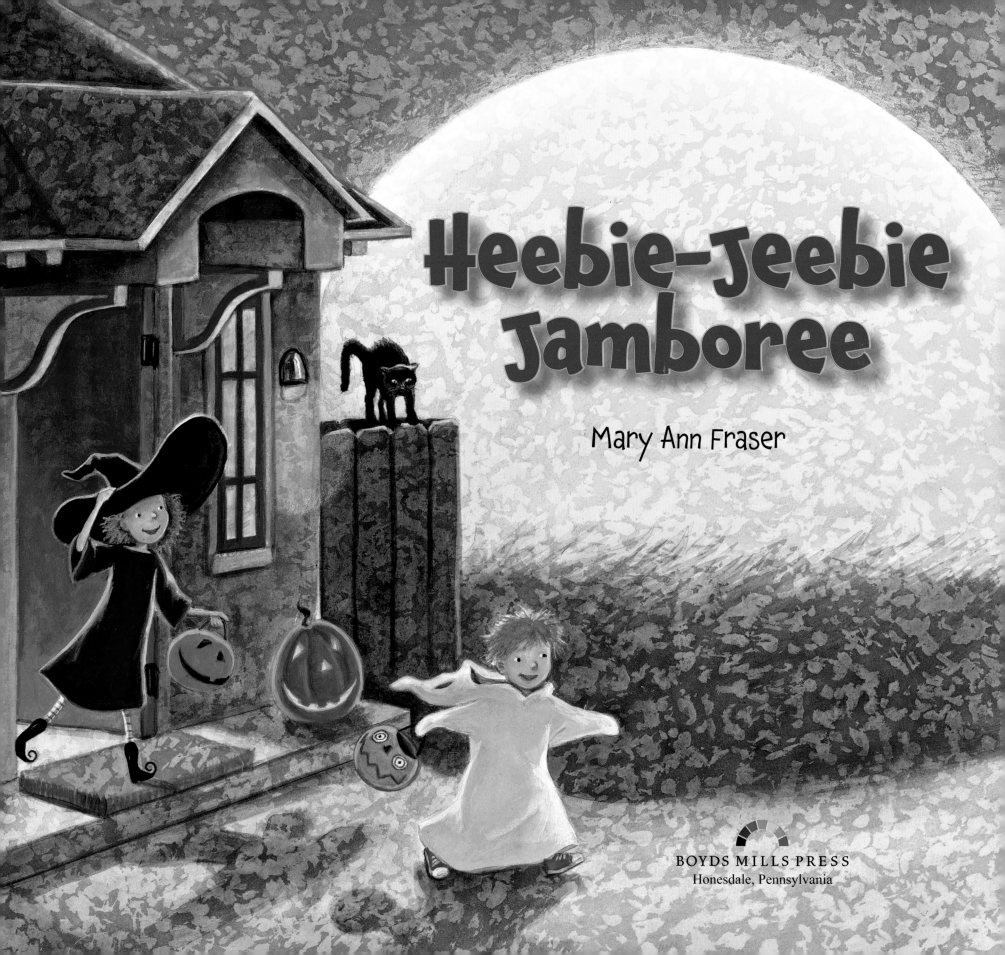

Heebie-Jeebie Jamboree

Mary Ann Fraser

BOYDS MILLS PRESS
Honesdale, Pennsylvania

Boyds Mills Press, Inc.
815 Church Street
Honesdale, Pennsylvania 18431
Printed in the United States of America

ISBN: 978-1-59078-857-8

Library of Congress Control Number: 2011920699

First edition
The text of this book is set in 20-point Chaloops.
The illustrations are done in acrylic.

10 9 8 7 6 5 4 3 2 1

CPSIA facility code: BP 312224

On Halloween night,
under a butterscotch moon,
Sam and Daphne pull two tickets
out of thin air . . .

. . . to the Heebie-Jeebie Jamboree.

"Tickets, please, if you've got the guts."

Sam and Daphne head right off
to see the sights.

Look! Warlocks bustin' brooms. Yee-haw!

Sip, slurp, burp.
Daphne stops to see which
witch's brew is judged
"The Slimiest."

"Don't miss the Fun Crypt," a barker calls.
"Daphne, follow me!" says Sam.

"Wait! Which one is you?"

"Have you seen my brother?"
"*Whoo?*"

Sam smells pumpkin pie.

Can Sam out-gobble the goblins?

Hooray! He wins first prize—
a jar of jelly eyes!

"Do you know where I can find my brother?"
"I see he is in for a bumpy ride,"
says Madame Mystère.

"Lost your mummy in the haunted house, little ghoul?"
"No, my brother," says Daphne.
"Try the mausoleum. Tonight's the big concert."

The Jamboree is fading away.
It's time for the departing to rest in peace.

But where is Sam?

Next Halloween,
under a butterscotch moon,
maybe you'll pull a ticket
out of thin air to the
Heebie-Jeebie Jamboree.